TIDES AT THE EDGE OF THE SENSES

Tides *at the* Edge *of the* Senses

NEW AND SELECTED POEMS

John Skapski

libros libertad
2007

First published by

Libros Libertad Publishing Ltd.
PO Box 45089
12851 16th Avenue, Surrey, BC, V4A 9L1
Ph. (604) 838-8796
Fax (604) 536-6819
www.libroslibertad.ca

Library and Archives Cataloguing in Publication

Skapski, John

The tides at the edge of the senses : new and selected poems / John Skapski.

ISBN 978-0-9781865-6-2

I. Title.

PS8637.K36T54 2007   C811'.6   C2007-903810-7

Design and layout by Vancouver Desktop Publishing Centre
Printed in Canada by Printorium Bookworks

This book is for Rivers Inlet and Millbanke Sound, two of the classic gillnetting areas on the British Columbia coast, and my personal favourites, but areas no longer fished; and also for the sockeye and the dog salmon we fished there, and the people who set those nets. Make your reasons, lay what blame there is where you wish, it hardly matters: the nets drift now only in memory, and the memory drifts. And this is for those who fished with us, but are no longer here to see this, but who also continue to drift through our collective recollection.

I do not know much about gods; but I think that the river
Is a strong brown god – sullen, untamed and intractable, . . .

The river is within us, the sea is all about us;
The sea is the lands edge also, the granite
Into which it reaches, the beaches where it tosses
It's hints of earlier and other creation; . . .

Where is the end of them, the fishermen sailing
Into the wind's tail, where the fog cowers?
We cannot think of a time that is oceanless
Or of an ocean not littered with wastage
Or of a future that is not liable
Like the past, to have no destination.

We have to think of them as forever bailing,
Setting and hauling, while the North East lowers
Over shallow banks unchanging and erosionless
Or drawing their money, drying sails at dockage;
Not as making a trip that will be unpayable
For a haul that will not bear examination . . .

—*T. S. Eliot, from "The Dry Salvages"* (Four Quartets)

Also by the author
In The Meshes (Sono Nis, 1970)
Green Water Blues (Harbour Publishing, 1978)

Some of these poems have appeared, in some form or another, and
not necessarily under the same titles, in the following:
Bridges (anthology), *Canadian Forum, C. B. C. Radio: Anthology,
C.B.C. Radio: Hornby Collection, Coast News, Contemporary Poetry of
B. C., Criteria, Expression, Fiddlehead, Going For Coffee* (anthology)
*Mainline, Mentor, Mundus Artium, New Orleans Review, New: West
Coast* (anthology), *Northern Light, Open Places, Otherthan Review,
Outstanding Contemporary Poetry, Poet and Critic, Poetry Australia,
Quarry, Raincoast Chronicles, Riverside Quarterly, The Far Point,
The Fisherman, The Otherthan Review, Trace, Voices International,
Ubyssey, Vancouver: Soul of a City* (anthology), *West Coast
Fisherman, Western Windows: A Comparative Anthology of Poetry
in B. C., Workshop, Yearbook of Modern Poetry,* and, happily
pre-posthumously, carved in the granite of the Fishermen's
Memorial located at Garry Point, in Steveston, the fishing village
which has been subsumed into Richmond, British Columbia.

Contents

DRIFT III

DRIFT IV

DRIFT V

DRIFT I

Coastline Blues: Two

Visions of the hustle that was
Dance among the black and leaning pilings
Like children playing in a cemetery: splash
Against shore, waterlogged cedar, and a memory
I continually fabricate, of the many packers
Always unloading salmon
Into a whirlpool of manpower and device.

Wharves, heavy with barnacles and time,
Teredoed through and through the days and nights,
Waterlog in the silences between
Shake cabins sinking under moss at waterside
And crumbling skeletons of half remembered boats
On this or that sandy shore or rock bound cove:
Where, now and again, my wake washes through
And re-invents men, motives, and machinery
Until those waves subside
And all that's past again lies calm.

All these relics. Rusting. Welds unbeading.
History hanging loose on failing rivets, hulls flaking
In the intertidal: masts nudging surface at lower tides
Like stray memories long after a finished affair.

Picking through the detritus beyond
These various storm-tide lines
Hunters of glass floats and other mementos
Work their way around another object
It's own tombstone, nothing more chiseled upon
Than what the sea deigns: only
Sand, lichen, and mind's invention
To state that once it was.

Entropy

I am, and go,
Like stone, downhill.

Such as seeks its own level
Moves, taking me with it.

All is time, and time
Is all: inexorable: winding down.

Say that I leap, and leap again
Into a current will never allow me.

Say this, but do not say
That I could not turn if ever I tried.

Equinox North:
Steering Grenville Channel

Take this watch, alongside, following north, as I
Toward the pale glow of a half-drowned sun:
A heading luminous through mind all false-dawn long,
Veiled like a mystery soon to be revealed,
Like the never that is all now and no time
That pale rainbow blizzard surely must conceal.

Endless repetition, imperfect parody of duplication,
Before and after smudged in one extended perception,
Merged the way water closes behind our passing.

All purpose reduced to belated excuse.
Whim of reason gone to seed
In such mind as is moment only.

In the clear between shadowings in of sheer fjord;
This passage. Reflection of sky almost phosphorescent,
Dreams and desires melted in moment of pure transparence
Before mind translucent with being only,
And the not being which is being, purely,
Blown before winds of a clouded undersurface sky
In this almost night of never quite light.

Color shadows of some northern aurora of sense
Dance that slow glide which shifts coldly
Within the pastel spokes of an ionized sight.

Stillness of night on snow too high for melting
Scatters us like moonlight faceted across wave tops,
Rapids of currents deeper and far closer than we understand.

Litany For Winter

My fingers numb in the ice-water. I've
Caught all that I can take this year.

The fish have gone: the run's dried up.
Put the nets away once more.

Always, come winter
The still warmth of lair
And the silent depths of salmon.

Netshed Notes: One

Mornings creak, straining at the night
They're moored to: awakening
Lurches to the surface.

Water slaps the planking by the bunk
But the dreamer has left the dream.
Slowly, sun burns mist off the waters.

Diesel smoke like perfume: recollections
Accrete about a small perception. All my controls
Are free. The machinery hums smoothly.

A crab scuttles across the bottom of these days.
The swells littered with jelly-fish sails,
Thin blue in the clear breeze.

Something other of emotion
Struggles in the nets. Waters, I sense,
Are somewhere overflowing.

And each year, harder,
That same instinct
Noses me seaward.

Netshed Notes: Two

Channels soon to flood with thaw:
The fry are moving in the gravel.

If I arrive there, the rain
Will greet me
Like an old friend.

North. Twisted in the long splice
Between day and night.

As the tides, some days
Fluctuate more than others. Set the lines tight.

Fog snakes over long ridge, into
Valleys and inlets I remember. I know
Only those some past tenses.

Dead rain on this flat calm.
The sodden cool of solitude.

Now Turn: Look

Turn to align with the turn of stars. I'm
Mesmerized to slow cartwheel of constellations.

Look for the ducks: look for the geese. Know
My boat's in the shadow of their arc

Spreading these waters to mirror
Their spreading wedge of air.

Ocean Monologue

I have no special hunger for those
The men I swallow. Nor grudge.

Merely the act of drawing into oneself
And those too close to the periphery topple in
Like trees undercut on some old riverbank.
Where wave closes over cabin, over them
Is merely the knack of being in the wrong place
At precisely the wrong instant.

No victory, no campaign nor effort
For there never was a war. Only
Weight across a surface so uncertain in support.

There is no siren song, no lure to the trap
More than waking lures to life.
Merely this act of inhalation, and
What rides the air is drawn in surely
As you are hauled across this face of planet.

What rides on water rides uneasy
Rides across the wet grain
Of where my water wills to go.

Requiem: For Hoss

Another one of us slips under the waves
Here, where ageing fishermen wait out the time
Away from time on the water,
Where we make peace with no longer setting nets.

Another one of us tangled in the mesh
Of that which nets us all in time,
Gone from the waters where our collective recollection
Still hunts down memories of fishing with each other.

Another one of us left looking back
At those of us who are still left, now looking
At the places where the rest used to be, their only memorials
Those thoughts that still have strength to swim upstream.

And you my friend, gone. Gone
From the times reminiscing together
About the times we used to fish together, and the others
Who fished with us and were no longer there to reminisce.

Spawning Cycle

These spring days grow longer
Until the dark comes closing.
What tides divulge, they once again conceal.

We're out to fish until — again —
It's time to be ashore.
Because the geese go by.

I'll be here with you
Till it's time to be alone: the way out
The way back, and all ways this one.

These Days

Sporadically, I get that sense
I'm beginning to feel fished-out.

The darkness of the night a bit more impenetrable
Where distances loom both close and far and neither
Hazy blur through that thin fog
Where detail disappeared upriver.

I remember older fishermen remarking
That night fishing was getting more difficult:

So this drifting a quarter mile of net
Through stands, dolphins and deadheads
Port and starboard channel buoys and markers
Rock jetties and piling studded wing dams:

A difficult dance getting more difficult
Under cover of such darkness.
Those things one knows far too well
Than to do with their eyes closed.

These nets of ambition older now
Ragged and torn with what was, and was
Little room left for what could be
Any mending not somehow longer worth the effort.

The old places aren't quite there any more
Sand bars have wandered like sand dunes
Channels cut, and re-cut elsewhere
As delta meanders. Old pilings, timbers
Rot and drag away in currents
Topple into undertows and undercut,

And a tide I feel taking me
Towards where the ones who are no longer here
Were last seen headed.

Undercut

Weather-shy, they call them:
The ones found always
To the landward side of a fleet,
Someone hostage between themselves and the sea.
Edgy at the first whine in the rigging.

Sometimes, it's that rogue wave,
That rock breaking suddenly by your bow,
Or that one time
When it seemed the boat would never right;
When maybe someone else didn't make it.
That time the sea drove your stomach high
Into your throat, and threw fear
Like a glass float blown into the shore grass
Far above some storm-tide line in mind.

Or, just a steady accretion:
Silting of small starts and heart-races,
Recollections of faces simply no longer seen,
Sedimentation of times you knew you didn't know.
Those flashes when you could see the catastrophe
And its end: yourself bloated, like a marker buoy
Floating at the end of your net.

These waves break, break, and break on
Wearing away, regardless how slow, until that day
They finally grind you smaller than the sea.

Waters, Next Year I'll Be With You

Walking the city's tamed wintering shores,
I keep seeing objects on the water,
Triggers of old memories
Stronger than I had any idea they were.

Deadheads bobbing inexorably
And the wash of water on sandy gravel,
Tide lines full of bark and detritus
And the dark cast iron throb of a diesel working

Wash through my mind, with a sense
Of some dim poignancy, as though
I'd set and forgotten some nets
(As fishermen are apt to do in dreams)
To tangle those fading recollections

Spawned of actions repeated until instinct,
And scenes watched over and over,
Circumstances that repeat themselves
Against a constant overlay of quest:
Some mythic sense of hunt, felt edgewise.

Ways North

Why these were the ways one chose,
Those long days north to spaces
Where man comes as but guest, and then
One received with but thin mask of courtesy

All this settling in, this homesteading
Little more than vagrant handholds
On sheer face of cold granite
Released, this interval, from years and years of glacier

Our trace but a widening wake
A parting, a surface spread thin in time,
Which closes silently behind
Almost before sound of this going stills.

Years on end one goes only to return.
North to thin harsh wisps of summers
Realizing just long after far too late,
That any choosing was but worked upon them.

DRIFT II

A Day in a New Life

I am inside a mud nest inside.
An oven bird returns, proffering
Assorted purple fire-hoses and orange-peel snakes.

Light pries open my minds like an oyster knife. Empty.
The harvest is over
And they're burning the stubble fields.

The fire-monkey splits the earth like a cocoanut,
Laps up the molten insides
And throws the husks into the sun.

We watch a moth on its back
Beating the dust off its wings beneath a street light.
Whipping the sidewalk into clouds of pollen with a limp flower.

Afraid to sleep. Ants
Might soldier us off in the night.
I watch the morning from inside an anthill.

A Shadow Of Skulls

I am peeled to my ribs
Like an orange; spread sectors
With a common source.

In the heat of the day
A bleached skull stares vacantly
At the desert sun, without squinting.

I do not see what it sees —
I only see myself looking out
From a hollow skull.

My head appears through a socket.
As I move, the skull winks stupidly
At a proliferation of skies.

Backstage Mind

Desire to meet that actor, the old pro;
In the balcony—many actors that I am.
A search of old theatres.

At the end of one empty hallway:
A trap door to the cellar. Found him
Among the best vintages: those aged, well-fermented moments.

Spoke of his greatest scenes, but the drunkard
Had confused them. Misquoted lines of himself
Which even I knew, for the first time.

Every scrap learned from him
Had been won at this expense: a slow leak,
Now only the empty cask remained.

Reputation, alone, has survived him.
I stand in this rain-barrel
Calling for a congress.

Chart Room

What has gone is all that is left.
I turn to each side: divining my pole.

The sounding-lines plummet inside:
Flowers unfurl to receive the dusk.
Here, the tides have stopped.

A reverse closure. I dismiss what is
And impose my own forms.

Years silt on years
In the delta regions of memory.
Slowly the channels fill.

It is a circle barbed with tangencies.
The center wheels outside: waiting.

I have walked for days among these stalactites
And met no one. Facing the past
We back clumsily into our futures.

We programme, then quickly forget.
My shadow moves off without me.

Conditional Incest

Do I contradict myself? Well then, I contradict myself . . .
—Walt Whitman

On the contrary,
I concur with myself.
You contradict yourself to agree with me.

All opinions —
Stones we throw into pools.
We reach beyond futility for even less.

In the copulations of infinity: another spasm.
Our time has come.
You change color like a hot star.

We are still sinking
Long before the rats have left.
Something picking at the locks.

Dialogue for an Accident

The last feints of the shadow-boxer
Echo through my senses. The axe passes:
I marvel at the smooth facets of the cleavage.

Convolutions settle like drawn entrails.
I believe I wait for the seagulls
Who pick the viscera from the puddles.

Like brakes
Locked in the last frantic skid,
We assume the positions of protection.

Understand: a looming girder bursts through
The splintered windshield of cognition.
All intrusions are unwelcome at the proper time.

As it is with marriage, a wedge halves my body.
The parts cannot be united
Yet are incomplete in themselves.

In the driver's seat, I have no control.
We careen
Toward the final cliff-railing.

Dissection

The bad actor lives in his re-takes: I
Live within that bad actor. On the tightrope
Between this impersonation and the next.

A commonplace of strange selves, an
Incremental split personality — masks with masks
Over their masks.

Every connection
Is a subsequent redefinition. There is merely
This frame, and perhaps the next.

From the foreign sphere of my being
I have broken all diplomatic ties.
The starfish retracts its limbs.

Beside myself: two strangers
Desiring no reconciliation. Others
Are also coming.

I only congratulate
That
I do not.

Dry-Spells

If I don't fail at first,
Perhaps the absent clouds will try;
One may soon know better for the worse.

Mouths open on the horizon
And enunciate the drought. Once more
He heaves handfuls of dirt toward them.

Our mirages memory raises: reverse
Of rain falling. Clumsy hands behind my eyes
Saran-wrap the vacant air.

Vulture layers of recognition wheel
With stones in their claws.
Lidless eyes watch from those fields.

Nothing changes. Ever. The only sound
Last guffaws of three parched trees: tumblers falling.
My tongue curls in my lap.

Dusk's Echoes for a Deaf Ear

Sunset smudges across the sky
Like oils slick on a morning puddle. The water: a hull
Streaked with the rust of recollections.

The sun a red bathysphere. Only what men inside?
Sinking past phosphorescent clouds:
Once more it doesn't return.

Night scrapes across us
Drawn by the potter's fingers on the wheel.
There is no escape, no attempt.

We find that to stop the world
We must first get off. Thunder, like a cat,
Rubs its back against the air.

All planets fluorescent yo-yos
Played crazily from the skies.
Somewhere deeper in space — a cretin giggle.

Colors exert themselves in a final surge:
The closing-out sale
Of some heavenly paint store.

Insinuations: One

They have evicted the apartments of memory
And sealed all the doors. I am alone
With my inquisitors.

Continuity hangs plumb:
An anchor. Come.
We are seduced by our futures.

Everything has been since the end —
Such is the curious stasis of change.
At last, we are all amphibian.

History returns, to confront
The rumor-mongering present: content
With parasite days. There were other ways.

If I have laid a cache of time
In the wastes of eternity — then
It *was* a waste of time.

Insinuations: Two

Sentenced to life
I wait for the commutation of death.
Perfumes, too, pollute us.

So much to execute
And so little reason: each act hangs
Like a carcass from a hook.

Frames of recollection project,
Like scenes from a train window.
The slow titration of understanding.

Scrap after scrap of insight
Lodges in the wastebasket of language —
Cards into a hat.

Tomorrow rustles behind us
Like a sheet of plastic in the wind:
The final nothing of all telescopics.

Insinuations: Three

All quests:
Monumentally futile
Monuments to futility.

Circles turn, and return upon themselves.
Some moibus of hunt.
We are emulsified in the past.

Meaning surrounds
Like cricket calls in the dusk.
There are no lighthouses, here.

Only a sense of the elusive remains,
A sense of dead of night.
Search for serendipity.

Insinuations of Time Without Place

Jellyfish blossom across the sky
Like paratroops.
The time of locusts approaches.

Only an eye impedes my vision.
The tin roof bristles like a seashell
At one's inner ear.

Through the droning afternoon
A dragonfly trails strands of silence. To my presence,
Let the environment adapt.

Mornings, termites' wings cover the ground
Like pine needles. At times,
We wear the gestures of others.

In the sky, I wheel above a scarecrow.
We evolve our contexts
By this process of unnatural selection.

Ivory Graveyard

All night long we hear the wind gnawing the bones.
Their marrow long since licked dry.
Time is also circular.

The vulture above,
We below; such effects
Abandon their causes.

There is a pile of bones in the room.
I call them conversation pieces
Rather because of the talks we have.

Knees up, we pay the final price.
Below, a puddle collects:
Soon the mice will be scurrying.

Somewhere: a Sargasso of bones.
A slow force draws me,
Gently. Perhaps clacking in the night.

Minotaur

There are no answers, only
Every day's reappraisals. I am in a maze
Of my own making.

Some days, one stumbles free.
You sit in the light for a while, and
The night comes like a silhouette against the sky. Always.

A man walks in an endless plain:
He avoids nothing, walks as he will.
We might all be pretenders to immortality.

Times: but I have been
Every fly
Under my thumb.

All else being changed, I may sometime return
Upon today. Only, behind me
Time gathers the strings.

Musical Chairs

In the highlands, among pines
A shadow
Stalks a new tenant.

There can be no contest — its prey
Grown lazy and familiar
Is out of shape.

By quiet shores, an unattached reflection
Courses the surface
Like a water-spider.

Behind this page: another hunter.
A struggle of one impaled upon words.
The barbs set.

Of Hardly Being There

Someone inside pushed his thoughts out: hopefully.
The words lay beached on the air,
Stretched like kelp on its dry frames.

What it was he did not know.
Someone she chose before him
Had known: still knew.

His hands reeled along a stone alley
Stopping to look in every door: all empty.
Even the sky stuttered.

The problem with his answers:
He asked the wrong questions.
A blind man forcing the wrong key.

Requiem: June 5, 1968

Again, the world buzzes
Like a fly
In an inverted wine glass: its
Pledges of non-recurrence.

The analysts gather: hindsight
Always upwind of events.
Caterpillars fall from a burning nest.

Personal freedom, as it sinks,
Is bailed
With the bell curve of elegies. Platitudes
Live another flurry of resurrections.

Mourners dressed in mourning
Lower the world into itself.
As usual, the hat is passed.

Synapse

In the catacombs behind my skull
A cave-man squats. Paints, in the torchlight
My views on all the walls: phosphorescent.

All distances across waters
Converge here. The questions?
Probably the only answers.

I gift-wrap all my apprehensions
And pretend to forget them. Anywhere.
Sooner or later the honest steal them.

Tides wash me up
On all
These shores.

It amounts, in a sense, to this:
Things are what they are,
And also what thought would have them be.

Tonalities of Being

All along we pursue
Things we pretend are not extinct. Thoughts, the gun-bearers,
Carry us into the bush.

At times, one is off the hook:
Busy signals for all callers.
You only believe we are in control.

The loose ends are all the like.
We tie the knots. What means?
Tomorrow is only one permutation of yesterdays.

Perhaps we are clouds in formation
Calling like ducks from evening skies:
Speak of motion, or say nothing.

The more we have,
The more we have to lose:
I am only breathing to myself.

Trapeze

Cantilevered over itself
The rope examines the abyss
Across which it stretches taut.

On a deep ledge
A miniscule man
Like a fly.

The tightrope walker stoops
To focus
Signals in an unknown semaphore.

In the flash he slips
Time to see a clown, like a baton,
Plummeting end over end upon himself.

DRIFT III

Address

You can find me, always
In this endless bay
Between here and there.

Moored to wharves
Held in place
Only by vagabond tides and currents.

Pull by, slow
As a boom under tow
Headed that other way
Toward a port I'm always leaving.

Beached

Instantaneously, the waters disappear.
Islands to peaks; reefs to ridges.
A new topography — high tide mark
Etched in kelp across the sky.

Jellyfish crack in the hot sun.

The depths' grip released. Red snappers
Puke out their air bladders, like obese tongues,
In obscene defiance.

The bends shriek in a head
I begin to feel exploding.

Claustrophobia's Just a State Of Mind

You'd call this small for a cheap hotel room,
Cramped for a prison cell, this
Cabin where I make my home
Wave after wave,

Month after month, surrounded
By all the paraphernalia of living
And technology of fishing,
Engine and instrumentation.

Spacious enough to me, this
Accordion of space
Three steps
From end to end.

Counting Down

Too many times, almost
You've walked away.

And no, I can't even begin to guess
What perverse gods you pray to,
What hexed amulet you rub,
Or what crank talisman you carry.

I watched your hatch covers that first time
Rising end over end above
The wobbling shadows of explosion.
Saw again, and wheeled the rudder
Toward the black smoke above
Those two other places where I knew you were.
I heard you and turned through those reefs
When you radioed, "Come and get me.
I just hit some fucking rock."
And heard of that time, when
Left treading leech-cold water
They chanced on you in the fog
At the last chance,
You catalogue of maritime disaster.

Too many times. Now
I detect a tinge of gasoline about you
And sense, somehow,
A rising water line.

Death, Mute

A past of dead ends —
Voyageur of dry river beds, he
Turns always upon himself
Turning on himself. Crying out
Words fall backwards
Into the wave-troughs of his absence,
Tumble over each other to form
What he has long since said.
Somewhere to return to return to, and
Nowhere to stay. Ever.

Silent:
Mouthfuls of words
Jammed at his teeth like logs
He waits
For the event
Which might break them out.

His life passed
In the wave of a hand.
Gravity unwinds itself
From about his death.

Dilemma

No means to say it. I
Can tell you this only,
Blinking like a beacon light
On this desolate night coast.

I flash you from nowhere
This message: simply, "Beware."
I see nothing, am certain of nothing,
Illuminate only this small circle.

I am in the eye of this storm:
Anchorage surrounded by wind. To leave
Would be madness, to remain
So much madder yet.

Endgame

For those fishermen
Beached on land
There is only the return
To the sea: more sea.

Gone
This way:
Lure, pleasure =
Habit, habitat.

Expatriate

Spoken to by the winds
And tides
Sun, moon and rain,
Wise in the ways of the earth:

Learned
Its language,
You might say.

Some trouble with the old one, though.

What the hell, not
So sure
There's anything left to tell
Anyway.

Experience

I carry with me at all times a pen, though I do not choose the fight with words: I am, simply, prepared. Inoculated against the disease.

Seagulls diving for small fish. Half their time spent hunting, half pursuing the victors.

In the beginning was the foraging for survival, and, in the intervals, rest. Quest becomes interval, and I for amusement stalk inside-out the game within me, regress to survival to escape resting.

Survival and search inside that cave man, the quantum of our inner shells, and the artist half all the artist one can be.

Fall Fisher: Two

There's a large bright ring around
That moon
Rising in my memory tonight.

Slowly, the eyes
Adapt to this dark
Perceive more, or else
Than stark light might reveal

Time, this teredo
Tunneling through the cedar timbered base
Of all our lives.

And memory, the empty wake
Of its hunger, the riddle
Of this riddling.

A propeller churning through
The liquid past: reverberations
Of recollections, through this hull.

Time floods back: another
Slack tide in being.
The moon hangs large on the horizon of age.

Here, below surface, where dreams converge
And currents sleep.

That I have been is but a memory.
This is all I remember now.

Getting Rid of You

Why are you always
Tangled in my web: must I
Pick you out to pick through
What it was
I came to fish these waters for?

Looking for somewhere
To set these nets
Without your swimming into them.

Some way
To lure you away
From the trap.

Sure, I'm glad
To find you around,
But every time I want to throw you back
You're back.

Guise: Invader

Slag in the desert
Haze in my eyes
Grit in my teeth

I am come: regolith

Stone sediment of stones.
Ash and dust in the skies
Pass through my pores,
Spores of mineral disease,
Spoor of harsh abrasion.

I am come to wedge
To argue, crack,
To insinuate past surrender.

Herring Prayer: Thought for a Rising Sea

Let them grind my body, mince it.
Let it be spread on neat little sea-canapés
And let the crabs and sea-lice pick my bones clean
With their pinkies curled.

Let it be a feast
Or a party, and
Let them pass me reverently about
Like some marine Eucharist

Just don't let it be now. No
Not just now.

Hooked

This is the year I quit, No
Question. Rolling here,
Winds rising, stomach too,
Giddy on the groundswell:
I'm through mainlining fishing.

Honest. Listen,
I'm off it for good: just
This one last set to make.

Hydraulic Notes

The beacon's light-swath
Outlines it against these wastes,
Like the blare of that fog-horn
Which erodes these moss-hung silences.

Above me: rippling: a surface
Which will accept no name. They
Move like glaciers in these depths.

Clouds slipstream
From the current-swept pinnacle of moon
Which juts from these night rapids.

Something swims along these frontiers.
Perhaps you saw it
As it curled by me, trailing
The back-eddy of tide I face into.

In the Instant Which Picks Mind's Locks

Come then, gentlemen: we have worried this too long.

—Kekule

I.   The grids are laid: meridians lace this globe.
       Let us go under: fracture matter to atoms, and
       The dissection begins.

II.   Fireworks burst high. Cell walls shrink.
       Metaphor stalks itself through the bloodstream,
       Its own antibody. No
       Words, now. Here
       In the long bright dream.

       The kaleidoscope regresses
       Toward that time
       When image falls suddenly
       Into line.

       Mechasm fingers its accordion.
       Compasses fumble for their poles.
       Overlays of all those tableaus in the lightning storm
       Rage through the flashing night.

III.   Sun beats warm on backbone: these lizards
       Bask on hot stones.

       Multicolor fish trail rainbows
       Through these tropical waters: that free-fall
       Through eternal hedonics.

Where flat plain meets sheer cliff
An electric current which intuits ends.
That elegance of anticipation.

IV.   Now, The final kick.
Some net in mind gives: The answer
Breaks upthought
To its spawning grounds.

Just For The Record

Hammer the dogs
Haul the logs
Pick fish
And reel net in:
Process, routine.

The hunt
Is exactly the hunt,
Is when we live.

Track cedar trails
And salmon spoor, watch
For their receding wakes
At all peripheries of vision.

Drop the lure: set
The net. Forget
The rest.

Life in the Bight of the Endless Rope

Not before it's time; no, don't let them take me
Before it's time. After that
I freely will my body to the bottom
And the fish who've given me my living.

But in all good time, and taste. Placed
There, an offering.

Not like those bad nights
Sweating and turning
When I see myself washed ashore:

When I endure in dreams
The treading of cold, deep water
Knowing that even that ship on the horizon
Can't get to me in time, that
The deep internal freeze will have set

As groin and sides leak the last heat
Like Christ ebbing on the cross,
Like moraine before growing glacier.

Listen

Crickets chirp the silences
Between these seconds.

The fish we were
Tickle the surface,
Eye on the fly.

Depth by echo: soundings
Flash on the screen
Where I have been. Yesterday
Is one appointment I shan't keep.

Between this day and the next
Stalks a deadly calm.
The edge of knife in wilderness.

Midwatch

I follow my star,
The pagan
Navigation light
Flashing from the stone altar
Of the shores.

I genuflect as I pass, and

Peering for the next guide
Which the water
Will raise up, I sacrifice

One match.

Monologue at Sea

I'll tell you, mate, I
Give this lecture often —
Every year —
To anyone who isn't here,
And you're one more
Who's no exception.

"Watch them move
On their boats, everything,
Swaying into holds always there. A grace
Born of custom. Easy going, here:
These men stumble ashore.

Brief existences at sunrise
Or sunset, wedged
In the arc of a rainbow.
Always
By surprise
And always alone.

Drop the hooks: set the nets.
There's worlds to be caught
Finning under that surface: only
What's captive of
These nets I set and set?"

Night Run: Guayaquil

Sunset gives way to early dusk.
Too low for first stars
Fishermen's lanterns appear.

Anchor chains shuttle by me. My only wish
To moor here
By one of many warm night-breezes.

Sail and arrive with twilight, I
Know you: night boat, night run.

Notice

I'll tell you
What I think I felt
Then, the way I feel it now, going
Wherever it takes me.

This much
I owe in explanation: you
Should at least consider.

No juggler: no carnie: no magician.
Newspaper of the senses. Today's
Fading report
Of yesterday's events. But

Don't quote me on the details —
They are inexact, subject to whim
And change without notice: only
Cloud forms on a windy day
Whirlpools in the rapids
And whatever it way
Just swam abreast by me.

One for the Flying Dutchman

Someday
I'm just pointing this boat west
And going

Till I'm out of sight,
Fuel, food, and
Time

Out of it all.

One More Go-Round

Well,
I've come this far:
Thirty years.
Maybe halfway,
The first swell or two
Of the crossing.

Already, you might say,
A bit seasick.

Other Fog Meditations

When I emerge from the dream, who enters?
Who knows? This strip
Of moibus, everyday of being.

Why is a question I can't know
The riddle that doesn't solve. There
Are many things that matter.

How many ways can we find
To say we're alone? And how long
Before we accept it?

Time the conjurer: I wish to keep alive
A touch of wonder, a hint of surprise.

But the fog: the fog. The fog.

Recurrences

Always, these strangest waters.
These first times.
Always courses plunging meteoric
From deep-space of possibility.

Each time, experience sneaks overboard:
The novice, worried and confused,
Left to cower at the back of within. These nets,
Always in the wrong place, I'm convinced.

And then: amazed
As I pull in the catch.
Amazed to find myself making love:
Perhaps writing this.

Salmon Cycle: Spring

Channels soon to bloat with thaw:
The fry are stirring in the gravel.

With echoes of ice that breaks in mountains,
Ice that cracks across streams,
Ice that shatters on the steel winter in my mind,
Comes the thaw: the means
Which fill the creeks to overflowing
The overabundance of spring:
This beetle, trundling gravel down the channels
Rolling the milky while melt-water
Down a nerve system of tributaries.

With the armor of ice that breaks after the freeze is done,
When the frost that turns to droplets
On slender new branches
Plunges into the stillness of ponds the ice has left
Rapping out its rhythm.
The message of fields of force,
The earth's re-alignment with the galaxies of spring,
Rattling into the gravel, deep, towards the eying eggs
Like a clear morning, this morse,
The message of instinct awakening.

> Now, the time, time
> *To stir*
> *Stir with the turning*
> *The turning of the aged toward death*
> *And regeneration, toward the test*
> *And the long night,*
> *The turning in order to return.*
> *And it is time, time*

Time for young to swim out toward old
Time for growth to sweep toward decay, toward
The soundless clash of ritual symbols
And the whisper of two generations passing in the night.

Scribe

He, the record keeper,
Chronicler of what passes
Through consciousness, here
To smear the instant through time
To prolong, fix
On the celluloid backing of memory
Those moments:
This very time.

Watch the scribe scrawl past
Toward present

Slowly receding.

Seventh Sea Adventist

Oh, you wide waters
With your waves brutal,
Currents inexorable, I
Who have no church
Must come to worship, here.

Saying nothing, I know
I'll never hear a sermon of platitudes
No cant, no dogma, no cautious morality
Just your relentless self.

Should I ever wonder
What course to steer.

Snowman

He moves toward the blizzards
He lives within. Between sunrift
And snowdrift.

Parka and vessel buoy him
In his wilderness, this
Immigrant to wastes: secure only
Within hostility.

The languages of emptiness he speaks:
Depths which capitulation allows. He waits
For the last step, the pitch forward
Into void white.
That final lungful of ice-water.

Things Unsaid

The forms simply demand, "Occupation?" and
You just print, "Commercial Fisherman."

You don't say, "I know they're down there
Waiting for me . . ." Or that

You piece together what happens in the sea
By what you interrupt with your gear: guess rabbit's worlds
By what you pull out of that damp hat.

Bad times, the stern rises and smashes back
With a boat length shudder, every wave,
Some mad judoist throws you on a wet mat
Again and again, all night long. Or, some times,
At that point long past exhaustion or caring
You're still out there in your stern, up
To your arse in scrap-fish and weeds
And only half your net picked up.

But it only seems that bad
When it's happening: some days it's
Flat beautiful calm and sunrise all day.
Good days and bad, and
Bad days you swear off it, list your boat for sale
Plan to become a prairie farmer,
Until it's safely past and you can laugh again.

DRIFT IV

Adrift

Words spoken wait for a time to be heard,
The stone trees topple by the lakeside.
She crouches on the stumps like the wind
And bays at no moon.

Marsh-grasses reclaim this wilderness.
The mobile of mirror turns. Always,
From the crowds surging through streets of mind,
A figure dodges: dead run.

Each day lower, heavier, the fog lies: like
Her loneliness: a leakage he caulks.
She has never seen the radar she is
Sweeping like a rainbow through the mists.

An Acceptance

Some years, the river floods.
We accept this.
The moon drifts
In the longshore current. Winters,
The river
May run backwards.

On the planet of the red dwarf
It is sunset all afternoon.

The river builds:
The river destroys:
The clock's hands
Move like driftwood.

The river fords itself.
Scrapes its underbelly on bedrock.

Now,
And I turn to water.
I must accept this.

Cold-Spells

Slower than the eye can see
A film of ice
Forms across my surfaces.

Frost-cracks heave —
Water settles
Under the steady freeze.

Glacier wakes
Inch across
The face of these centuries: easily.

Crevasses jam shut on the past.
The fist of a new ice age
Closes in on molten core.

Drifting

Again, ennui arrives. Squats
Like a hulk rotting on some beach.
Only a succession of tides,
Release of silt: rusted nails
Letting go of ribs. And the insects
Burrowing all our planking.

Riding the swell, the ship bobs.
Moored to a hesitancy, a gentle
Fluctuation. The helmsman of doldrums
Omniscient in cipher realms.

Fishers of hook-less lines, web-less nets,
Intent for the bob of cork that tells.
The snow settles, and settles: slush
Lies like a scum. A bird overturns.

Inside, one by one,
The navigation lights expire.
There is drifting. Just drifting.

Equinoxes

A soft pulse in consciousness, like the wind
Which stretches new sails. Deep inside
The thoughts that hold the tacks
Across all those surfaces I sail upwind.

Zephyr days and times of storm: a sea anchor
Slipping through the waters that I am.

The stars we sail clear nights by:
Beacons which overwhelm all our voyages.
The start and completion, only,
Marked by lighthouses.
Always alone on deepening waters.

All the autopilots set: mornings
Find one at the tillers. What suns rise?

I heel
Before the onslaught of more perceptions,
Knifing this spray
Before me.

Headwaters

I

Time calibrates these years
In cycles of spawning runs.

Like musty netsheds
His dreams
Hang stuffed with meshes: carelessly
Planking peels from the ribs.

Blood pulses with the tides.

II

The surfaces
Of the fisherman's recollection:
A clutter of driftwood. In
The depths, silt settles.

Water
Recurs feminine:
That she spurned him is forgotten.

A whirlpool slowly siphons time.

III

Currents corrode currents.
The onwash breaks on iron rocks.

He wakes the days it drizzles —
Caulks the open seams in existence:
Rot tangles in his nets.

Twilight finds him turning home
At the upper reaches of this tributary.

The shore breezes turn back to the sea.

Reflections Behind the Revolving Door

In the room of dark mirrors
Eyes reverse their sockets.
Searchlight beams patrol the skies, here
Where no moon rises.

The mad gunner all night
Shoots clouds into the clouds. Scaffoldings
Collapse within, as black light
Illuminates a burning horizon.

This land of no co-ordinates,
The hunter
Becomes the carcass of his prey.
Inside, he waits for himself.

A dismissal of mirrors.
Images shrink, dead run,
Past the vanishing point
Where their many unlikenesses meet.

Riding Lights

I

In there, it is always night.
In solitude,
This lapping at the base of his skull.

He is so many sunrises.
So many sights
Acid-etched in recollection.

Often the wind, or perhaps
A scattering of rain.
A rise in humidity.

Knowing he can't
He understands water; feels it
In the currents inside him
With the hands of the blind.

Too many times
He has drowned:
And will again.

II

River eddies by the hull.
The anchor line stalks its locus.
The fisherman sleeps his sleep.

Far deeper than emotion
An arm emerges from the undertow,
Clutches the bellying wind.

An arc of geese
Against the setting sun.

The times
We feel it all capsizing:
Heeled hard over
In unseen whirlpools.

Rip-Tide Responses: One

I

One by one
She drives the days, like stakes,
Into the fish-trap upstream,
Playing to a rheotaxis born
Of the flow of their intimacy: the
Stability of sea-anchors.

II

The hook sets in jaws I swallow.
Always, it is exactly too late.

Somewhere, a breaker surges,
Shouldering the present on its crest:
Inexorably, days gain momentum.

He moves by like an outbound ship.
A life-ring forced out of reach.

Rip-Tide Responses: Two

I
Her words rattle an old rhythm
Through this millrace — the beat
Of a pebble's ricochet.

II

We exchange our fluid ballast
Like canal locks, spilling
One event into the next: waters
Which never restate themselves.

Underfoot
A surface of vertigo
Too thin to rest upon.

Floods burst these dykes.
Their actions stratify like sandstone.

Rip-Tide Responses: Three

I

The river slows: sediments
Precipitate from one more relationship.

The cliff: above, below: runoff and undercut.
Winds strip topsoil from the land.
He becomes another extinct creature
In the cautious ecology of her feelings.

II

Ripples across still water
Echo her outward: planets
Weave their concentric orbits
Into a soft-edged memory
Against the background of her blurred night.

Gyroscopes steady into these currents.

Rip-Tide Responses: Four

I

Out of a well-head of tributaries
We emerged into the river, which,
At some careless point
Becomes — simply — ourselves.

An osmosis of gestures
Through the porous membranes of recollection.
Seepage of dreams drips from stone.

He displaces just so much emptiness:
Enough to buoy him in her feelings.

II

Love, the old chameleon,
Fits himself
Over one more camouflage.

The Half-Tides

I

The word is the end of thought: the record,
The end of inspiration. I erect a tombstone
For this realization.
At the end it will commence again.

Low tide: the shoals surface.
Mariners adjust their memories.

II

There is little to say. A few short sentences.
Sound to exist only as sound.

The hitch-step in the march of waves.
Scarcely submerged, the rock, the deadhead,
Lie in wait beneath a thin film of surface. We see
Only these signs of presences which are not.

No more than these capitulations: ripples
Of a stone thrown again and again. Wakes
Forever distancing from their source.

III

All the springs of being have unwound.
Time relaxes — waiting for the next flurry.
A shadow stalks through the charred trunks

Of many burned-out mountainsides.
A new stand grows for the next fire.

Winds rattle through the dry sand-grasses. Waiting
For the silence that reveals, the tide that doesn't.

This River, Again

Abandoned: the booming grounds
Of forgetfulness. Return
Of a dusk heron.

In the silt below
Chains search out shapes of net.
We relinquish nothing. Ever.

Ease, like the slack at high tide.
The past settles on the water
Like mosquitoes among the reeds.

I watch
The wake
From where it vanishes.

Waterfalls

His world will be flat —
The ant rides a leaf toward the cataract.
You plan parties
To entertain your favorite fears.

To reach the ladder
Fish play the fishermen
Against one another.

There are times when only the unreal
Seems possible. But times.
The pawn directs through the player's eyes.

Over these falls
Even the water rides in barrels.
Nights, we feel
Gnawing at our moorings.

DRIFT V

Black Hole/ Ice Age Meditation

Eternal hibernation inside silence
Where the snow never stops settling,
White black in this absence
Of even the dimmest polar glow. A thin trickle
Of identity, the almost stream
Carved under this old glacier, waits
To discover itself
Should the thaw ever arrive, ever, here
By this long dead star.

Past all past, beyond even beyond
Headed black-side from all else
Where time receding shows less than mere speck
And space isn't even that first nanosecond long.

Beware of Strangers Setting Nets

My contact with your society of scales and gills: I
Have met those of your almost predecessors
Vanished in my nets (grand-aunt Sal
Uncle Al, and all the rest)

Your trader: bead bringer
Still making my raw deals with you,

My fine finny friends.

Divorce and the American Reloaders' Association

When that piggy-eyed little stranger
Poked his grubby stubbled face
And that wavering thirty-eight
With those copper-jacketed slugs
[Shining large, and as bright
As the berserker in those eyes]
Around that deserted corner,
I felt, finally, a real fear:
Frozen. Like the moment, deep
In my imploding stomach: noticed, then
Some urine dribbled down my leg.

Almost like the time she said, "Dear,
I've got something to tell you . . ."

And I waited that eternal moment
While glacier grew around me,
And her words shuddered home,
Deadlier then than if she had been there
To pull that trigger for that vanished runt.

Double Indemnity

When my then wife, after ten years
Told me from next to nowhere
That she was leaving, and had another man
Nothing worked on my fishboat anymore.

It was like I'd lost all my anchors
On a stormy night in shallow water.
My engine sputtered. The clutch slipped. The autopilot wobbled.
Planking started leaking, and even the stove
Wouldn't burn clean. It seemed
Even that fucking boat was on her side.

I wanted to drop the flywheel
Through her skull, stuff her full
Of burned-out clutch plates, drive her fatally off course,
Pump her up with greasy bilge water, and blacken her
Inside and out with that goddamn soot,
While I ran the propeller in sharp circles
Through that other man's entrails.

But I fixed and sold that traitorous fishboat,
Got another one, gave her that divorce, and set back to sea.
I couldn't work out any foolproof way, somehow
To burn myself up, and still collect the insurance.

Green Water Blues

All day that engine roar bores
Into his long dieselled senses.

Waiting for sleep to erase
This vertigo of awareness:
Riding above the bilgewash sloshing.

Late that afternoon he goes mad
Staving off madness. The boat
His oceans rock inside his skull
Heels closer and closer to capsize.

Kyuquot Dream

There's a huge slide scooped out
Of that night mountainside
Steep and high along this shore,
Rising into the full moon dawn.
We're running the outside down.

High on the hogback
One tree spars out sharp and taller. Near:
Those silent radars, domed and white. Waiting.
Watching. Thin filaments spidering out
That x-ray web which simply touches. They
Note our motion and continue, turning
In their phosphorescent dream.

I sense our voices guyed high
In that circle of radio-towers nearby,
Ringed desolate like some new Stonehenge.
Occult electrons flitting like bats or swallows
Beneath the night constellations
Pin-wheeling above. Time floods back
Through all those similar times.

A harsh roar breaks
From under cabin floorboards.
Like a float-plane driving off the water.
Diesel breaking that stillness
Mind and motion can gently merge.

Long Snow

Snows echo lightly through the last dry leaves hanging.
Somewhere, drifting, sounds of a lone dog's bark
As city retreats behind a white silence spreading.

End taxes. Abolish death. Repeal the laws of gravity!
And why so serious, my beloved one? Set me a place
To curl warm beside the hearth fires of eternity.

Do not confuse yourself. Do not permit words too much.
Remember, they are but echoes between ourselves hanging
On the quiet edge of a winter whose meaning drifts always.

We've been some way down those dark tunnels we must again.
Updrafts of a flitting white waver between one-ness and two
Blinding the tracings which some alone find time to follow.

We will awake in the morning buried feet deep in bed,
Shake back the banks of sleep like wolves rising,
Turning to each other within the warmth which separates us.

Losing Way

They say Ziggy lost his nerve
The time that wave
Drove his windows, piece
By jagged piece,
Into the cabin wall
Behind where his face used to be; say
You could make out his shadow
Daggered into that wood.

Now he wasn't the only one. No.
But it's a strong story
And it isn't all that hard to guess ·
Why no one really blames him.

You know whatever accidents conspire
To trap a salmon in your nets
Would just as ready wrap you
On your drum, drag you over in the net,
Spill you, trip you, flip you, lose you
In the wavering fathoms between surface and seabed:

You die a little, so many times,
Until there's no one left to kill.

Revenge is a Dish Best Served

"And then when the sonofabitch
Came home one night so plastered
He could hardly stand up straight
Well, I took him to the top
Of the basement steps, and
Helped him fall down. And
Then helped him up the stairs
So that I could help him fall again
And again. And again.

Kept that up until the bastard
Just couldn't make it up the stairs no more.
Black and blue he was all over:
Like he'd been thoroughly kicked and beaten.
By some gang in a barroom brawl.

Well, when he woke the next day
He was so damn sore he couldn't move
But couldn't remember a thing," she said proudly.

Perhaps he couldn't recall, but she still remembered
Her broken jaw from some other drunk of his.

Rondo

Drift

Throw away that which you impose on the world.
Who are you, to dictate terms to the universe?

Just a leaf on the surface,
A twig in the current. Drift.
Drift that purposeful drift.

Urn

In the patient dirt, these shards
She pieced together
In a way beyond what I had been.

Curious: mere archaeology
But the task completed
Nonetheless, that vessel restored.

Scale

The sea can teach such lessons as
One might never live to learn.

Love Song

She once was.
Say that.

Say it, and know, now
That's really all there is to know.

Sailor's Lament

You have looked into the depths of ocean
And said there is no soul there, where
The waters swallow men whole
And often alive: engulf house and hearth
In this liquid maw of survival. But
I am Jonah returned
From out the belly of that whale.

And what would you know of it, you
Who would serenely spread a picnic cloth across
Quietly slipping us under like sandwich crumbs?

Say That I Wait

Say that I wait to possess
The locus of your body, through these hands
The way the patterns of those webs I mend
Can overlay across unwatchful mind,

And say I wish to recognize you
As tide knows moon which draws it
As land knows that rise and fall;
Your ebb and flow perceived beyond flesh.

Say that, and know that you
Will continue to come and go within
As surely as we understand salmon
Returning ever to some point dim in time.

These Small Hostages We Hold

Curious, the ways we work, to keep holds
On each other, often after reason for holding
Has long since gone to seed.
"Yes, I have those poems of yours to copy
And I still owe you one belated birthday dinner,"
She informs me, just as I
Make a mental note of her book yet to be returned
And that appointment still to arrange.
This ultimate balancing
Of our overdue accounts.

Finding ways to close in on one another
Now we no longer live together.

And what dark politics behind these small hostages
We continue to abduct?

The small liberties and caresses, which
Will lead to yet another round of love making
As the larger carousel winds slowly down.

What Moves Behind Those Eyes

What moves behind those eyes,
Those eyes that move and in moving,
Without seeing fully, relay messages
Lost somewhere between retina and cortex:
Dissipating in transition from focus to feeling.

What moves behind those eyes,
Within a vision circling some dark concern, entrance
Curtained off by a fog somewhat between
Inattention and preoccupation: a fog thin, a mist
Insubstantial, but barrier however named.

What moves behind those eyes,
As they move through this clear day, crisp
With sun bright off sharp mountains, and
New snow on high ridges: a day begging for attention
As eyes move alongside this beach
Where other eyes move, those here for the seeing.

What moves behind these eyes
My eyes which could just as easily,
One supposes, be yours. Anyone's.
And what do they hunt, here in such unmapped interiors?
Do they chart position and magnitude of events that loom
Large, but soon subside, like icebergs melting
And slowly toppling; or like continents rising and
Subducting, to rise again some other place
Some other geo-millennium. Plans of the ephemeral in memory
Scrabbled on tissue forever crumbling at the touch.

What moves behind those eyes
Turning over events, courses of events,
Loves, opportunities, the done and the undone
Inspecting as though some day all would suddenly
Be revealed, all right and wrong separated cleanly.
Rubbing time's mementos like some amulet of arcane power,
The fingering over and over of worry beads
In and old man's worn and working hands.

What moves behind those eyes
Trapped between vision that is mere perception
And the seeing which is clear understanding, that
Which may make sense of a life not fully understood
Understanding always that the one enduring feature
Is life's ability never to comprehend itself quite fully.

What moves behind those eyes
Which moves also in sleep, when retinae
Are lit from inside only: which in moving
Appeases that which causes such to move
Without quite satisfying: which by moving
Is able to rest, knowing there is ahead only
More of moving and more of resting.

What moves behind those eyes
Eyes locked in an interior unsettled,
Not quite stormy, times of days of troubled weather
Where birds wheel thick and shrieking
Wheeling to land only to rise and wheel again: times
Of portents, of signs seen clear but clearly ambiguous.

What moves behind those eyes
That pass, and hitch-step in their moving
Meeting these. Those eyes so like your eyes,
Where I have looked for warmth or certainty
Or perhaps a trace of that which lurks cautiously
Within the darkness there, seeing only
That restless question reflected. What moves?
What moves behind those eyes, all eyes?

ABOUT THE AUTHOR

I was born in London England during the end of the war, Hitler's V2 rockets/bombs were still falling. Especially while in utero, my mother is wont to recall. My father was one of the Polish free army in Exile and, like so many of them, he married an Englishwoman and did not return to Poland, which was too far behind the Iron Curtain. Post war Europe being not much better off after the end of the war than during, they headed for South America (where my mother had been the British equivalent of a CUSO worker prior to the war) and wound up in Paraguay, in a small town 30 kilometers from the Argentine border. Semi-tropical, with banana and citrus growing in the yard. Pet parrots and toucans on the porch. You had to be careful not to step barefoot on the toads when you went to the outhouse at night. Dirty and backwards. Snakes, tarantulas and all manner of opportunistic insects. I only wore shoes to church on Sundays. It was like the wild west: people rode horses, and drove buckboards. When they left town they strapped on their sidearms. There was no electricity, running water, or paved roads. The first car through town ran over my dog: he'd never seen one before. All in all, a great place to be a kid. Until I was eight I was home schooled, but by then my parents had figured that prospects weren't all that promising there either, so we wound up in Vancouver, and then to Steveston.

Fifty percent of the people I went to school with there were Japanese, which felt comfortingly like Paraguay, and fifty percent again got involved in the fishing industry at some point. Steveston was a busy, booming, bustling, fishing and cannery town. By the time I was fifteen I was deckhanding on salmon gillnetters in the summer. After I graduated I got to working as a Mate on a fish packer, and also putting in time at the salmon canneries. I went to UBC, joined the weightlifting team, and got about half way through an engineering degree. I didn't dislike it, but I was more interested in poetry and such, so I switched over into Honours English and took some writing courses. With a fellow called Yates: J Michael, as I recall.

I was also captivated by fishing, and about then I managed to start gillnetting on my own, by way of fish company rental boats. There was quite a group of us from Steveston starting up at the same time. I'd fish while I could, and then go back to the cannery work to pay off the company store. By the time I was done with a masters degree in Creative Writing and it was time to look for work, fishing was working out a lot better. I had bought my own boat. As well as a house. We fished from late spring through to early autumn and had the rest of the time to travel and relax. We fished hard, played hard. Academia seemed too much trouble and not enough fun.

I moved up coast to a waterfront home in Pender Harbour, with my boat tied to the dock outside. A great place, the harbour, with some seventeen miles of waterfront inside. Bought cedar logs from a show on Thormanby Island and salvaged smaller logs from the Malaspina straits to build myself a new wharf. I remember going out after dinner in the spring and coming home late at night with salmon I'd netted half an hour from home. A view of Whiskey Slough and Dunc Cameron's fish packers. But life is full of surprises: I wound up divorced and in Vancouver and headed back to school. Law was the only faculty that would have me without going back for qualifying courses, so there I went. But when I wasn't taking courses, I was still gillnetting the coast, from the Straits of Juan De Fuca to the Queen Charlotte Islands, and up behind the Alaska panhandle. School and salmon fishing were always a good fit.

Eventually I set up shop on my own in Steveston, and found I was doing law for the fishermen I knew, as much as anything. But they weren't there in the summers, so it was still possible to head out fishing, though for protracted seasons. Twins came, taking the time children take, along with extended El Ninos, falling salmon prices, and government meddling with the industry. It gradually made more sense to stay home with my family and practice law than to chase after fish which got harder to catch and were worth less when you finally got them. By then I'd had a chance to take my kids out fishing and provide them some memories to furnish their childhoods with. In all, I've spent over thirty-five years in the fishing industry. I still think of myself as a fisherman, one like many of the older ones I knew when I was starting out, who had shore jobs to fill in the lean years.

Turning sixty finds me living in a place overlooking the Steveston dike where I played as a youth, with a view down the mouth of the Fraser across many of the spots I fished over the years. At night, I can see the Sandheads lighthouse flashing: and the channel buoys. Playing old-timers hockey after I learned to skate to keep involved with my son when he took up the game as a five year old. Going to my forty-five year high school reunion next week, though I've never attended any of my degree granting ceremonies (you've got my address—mail it in). Wondering just what the hell retirement may be about, and what other turns are in store. Though I know there's some poems waiting out there for me.

—*John Skapski, 2007*